This book belongs to

_____

THE AMAZING MUFFIN SEARCH

DISNEY'S

READ and GROW LIBRARY

Published by Advance Publishers
Winter Park, Florida

© 1997 Disney Enterprises, Inc.

Written by Susan Cornell Poskanzer   Edited by Bonnie Brook
Penciled by Edwards Artistic Services   Painted by Jim Crouch
Designed by Design Five
Cover art by Peter Emslie
Cover design by Irene Yap

ISBN: 1-885222-80-7
10 9 8 7 6 5 4 3 2 1

Early one morning, Grandma Duck opened all the cupboards in her kitchen. She had a plan . . . a big plan.

"Get up, Gus," she said. "Rise and shine! It's time to start!"

4

Gus Goose rubbed his eyes. He was still tired from the day before. Gus had spent the day cleaning his shoelace. Then he had carefully hung it out on Grandma's clothesline and watched it dry. That was the part that really had worn him out. In less than a minute, Gus had been snoring in the hammock and hadn't awakened until just now when he heard Grandma calling.

"Today's the big day," said Grandma.

Gus scratched his head, trying to remember what was so big about today.

"I forget," admitted Gus. "Just why is today the big day?" he asked Grandma.

"Because today we are going to bake a magnificent muffin that wins a prize at the county fair!" said Grandma, throwing *old* pots to the left and *new* pans to the right onto the kitchen table.

"Come on, Gus!" said Grandma. "Let's get going!"

"OK, OK," said Gus.

"What kind of muffin should we make?" asked
Grandma, looking at her cookbook. "How about cherry?"

"Mmm, nice and *sour*," said Gus.

"How about banana?" asked Grandma.

"Mmm, nice and *sweet*," said Gus.

"How about orange juice?" asked Grandma.

"Mmm, nice and *wet*," said Gus.

"How about peanut butter?"

"Mmm, nice and *dry*," said Gus.

"I know! I've got it," said Grandma. "We'll make
a cherry, banana, orange juice, peanut butter muffin.
That will be perfect!"

Soon Grandma and Gus were stirring a huge bowl of muffin batter. Then Grandma poured the batter into a big pan. Gus opened the door, and Grandma plopped the *cold* pan right into the *hot* oven.

The door closed and the marvelous muffin began to bake. It smelled wonderful!

Everyone on the farm sniffed the air, wondering what smelled so good.

Chip and Dale smelled the muffin, too. "Mmm," they said. "That smells good!"

Meanwhile, the muffin rose and rose. It got bigger and bigger. Just as it was about to burst out of the oven, Grandma opened the door and took out the most gigantic cherry, banana, orange juice, peanut butter muffin anyone had ever seen in the whole wide world.

"Oh, my!" said Grandma.

"I bet we'll win first prize at the county fair," said Gus.

The muffin stood so *tall* that Grandma and Gus felt *short* beside it. It was so *fat* that Grandma and Gus felt *thin* beside it.

Peering through the window, Chip said, "Now how can we get a piece of that muffin?"

"Hmm! There must be a way!" answered Dale.

The muffin's wonderful smell traveled through the air.

It went all the way to the Woodchucks' campground, where Huey, Dewey, and Louie were hiking in the woods.

"Do you smell what I smell?" asked Huey.

"Yes!" answered Dewey and Louie. "Grandma is baking!"

In minutes, Huey, Dewey, and Louie were at Grandma's farm.

"Wow!" they said as they got their first peek at Grandma's giant muffin.

"You're just in time!" said Grandma, kissing the three boys hello. "This muffin is for the contest at the county fair. You can help us load it onto the truck!"

"Sure," said Huey, Dewey, and Louie.

They *pushed* the muffin.

They *pulled* the muffin.

18

They *lifted* the muffin.

They *lowered* the muffin. And finally they tied the muffin tightly to the top of Grandma's truck.

"Great job!" said Grandma. "But it's *hot* outside. Come inside for some *cold* lemonade."

"Hmm," said Chip. "If that muffin went *up* on the truck..."

"There must be a way to get it *down*!" said Dale.

Chip and Dale called to the farm animals.

"Do you want a treat?" Chip asked them.

"Just follow us!" said Dale.

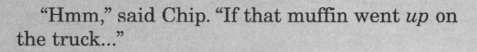

"Sorry to rush," said Grandma. "But I think we should leave for the fair!"

Then she hugged the boys.

No one noticed Chip and Dale as they scurried up a tree with pieces of the muffin. No one saw the farm animals quietly munching on their portions of the delicious muffin.

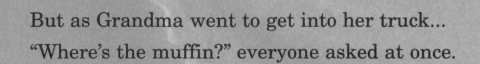

But as Grandma went to get into her truck...

"Where's the muffin?" everyone asked at once.

"Gone," said Gus.

"But where could it have gone?" said Grandma. "Muffins don't just walk away."

"Don't worry, Grandma!" said Huey.

"We'll help you find the muffin," said Dewey.

Huey, Dewey, and Louie spread out all over the farm, looking for the lost muffin.

They looked *up*.

They looked *down*.

They looked *near*.

They looked *far*.

They looked *high*.
Then they looked *low*.

They looked *over* things. They looked *under* things.

They looked all over the farm. But they just couldn't find that marvelous missing muffin anywhere.

"My marvelous muffin is lost," said Grandma *quietly*. "Now we won't win a prize at the fair. Now we won't even get to the fair!"

Big, fat tears streamed from Gus's eyes. He cried *loudly*.

Suddenly, Huey, Dewey and Louie had a great idea.

"Get out the *old* pots!" yelled Huey.

"Get out the *new* pans!" yelled Dewey.

"Get out the flour and eggs," yelled Louie.

"Get out the cherries, the bananas, the orange juice, and the peanut butter!" the boys yelled together. "Woodchucks to the rescue!"

Suddenly, Grandma's eyes sparkled. She knew what the boys were thinking.

"Gus, we're going to bake another muffin," said Grandma.

"We are?" asked Gus.

"Yes, we are!" cried Grandma.

Soon Huey, Dewey, and Louie were mixing cherries, bananas, orange juice, and peanut butter. Grandma and Gus were mixing huge bowls of muffin batter.

When they were done, Gus opened the stove door and Grandma plopped the *full* pan right into the middle of the *empty* oven.

Then Grandma, Gus, Huey, Dewey, and Louie all sat back and waited, while the air filled again with wonderful muffin smells.

"That muffin smells good," said Chip, "but I'm full."

"I'm stuffed," said Dale.

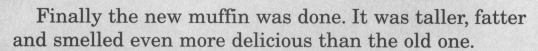

Finally the new muffin was done. It was taller, fatter and smelled even more delicious than the old one.

They all *pushed* and *pulled*, *lifted* and *lowered*, and finally tied the second muffin tightly onto Grandma Duck's truck.

"Thanks, boys," said Grandma as she got into the truck with Gus. "We couldn't have done it without you!"

"Good luck, Grandma," said Huey.

"I bet you'll win first prize!" cried Louie.

And sure enough, that's exactly what she did!

As for Chip and Dale, they were starting to feel a tiny bit hungry again. They grinned at each other, knowing they would have another tasty snack the very first chance they got!